Sara is at her grandfather and grandmother's house. Sara loves her grandfather and grandmother. She loves their little house and garden, too.

Grandfather and Grandmother have a big brown dog and a little black and white cat. The dog's name is Bruno and the cat's name is Lucky.

Sara likes playing with Bruno, or sitting quietly with Lucky.

Sara often helps Grandfather and Grandmother in the house and garden. Grandmother grows lots of flowers and vegetables in the garden.

Grandfather cooks the vegetables for their meals. They're really good. Grandfather is a good cook.

"I'm growing turnips this year," Grandmother says. "There's a really big turnip in the garden. I want to pull it out of the ground today. Your grandfather can cook it for us this evening."

She puts on her old coat, and Sara finds her coat too.

Can I come with you?

Grandmother and Sara go out.
Sara can see the turnip at the end of
the garden.

"Grandmother, it's enormous!"
Sara says.

Grandmother starts pulling.
The turnip doesn't move.

Can I help?

Go and find your
grandfather first.

Sara comes back with Grandfather. Grandfather puts his arms around Grandmother and they both pull, but the turnip doesn't move.

Now can
I help?

Grandmother takes her coat off. Sara puts her arms around Grandfather. Grandfather puts his arms around Grandmother again.

Grandmother says, "One... two... three... PULL!"

They all pull, but the turnip doesn't move.

Bruno the dog comes into the garden.

Look, Grandmother, Bruno wants to help!

Bruno pulls Sara's coat. Sara puts her arms around Grandfather, and Grandfather puts his arms around Grandmother.

"One… two… three… PULL!" says Grandmother.

They pull and pull, but the turnip doesn't move.

"Lucky, come and help us," says Sara.

"A cat? What can a cat do?" asks Grandfather.

Lucky pulls Bruno's tail. Bruno
pulls Sara's coat. Sara puts her arms
around Grandfather, and Grandfather
puts his arms around Grandmother.
They pull and pull.

"I think it's moving a little,"
says Sara.

A little mouse runs past. It stops, and then it pulls Lucky's tail. Lucky pulls Bruno's tail and Bruno pulls Sara's coat. Sara pulls Grandfather and Grandfather pulls Grandmother.

It's moving now!

The turnip quickly comes out of the ground. Grandfather, Grandmother, Sara, Bruno and Lucky all fall down. They are laughing.

Look at it!

That evening, Grandfather cooks chicken with turnip.

The next day, Grandfather cooks sausages with turnip.

Grandfather cooks turnip every day for a week. He and Grandmother make turnip meals for all their friends.

"I like turnips," says Grandmother, "but I want to grow something different next year."

Turnips and other vegetables

Turnips are vegetables. We grow vegetables and eat them.

Some vegetables, like turnips, grow under the ground.

Some vegetables grow on plants above the ground.

Some vegetables are good in salad. You don't need to cook them.

Lots of vegetables are good in soup.

Do you like vegetables? Are there some vegetables that you don't like?

Activities

The answers are on page 32.

Can you see it in the picture?
Which three things *can't* you see?

cat sky flower garden girl vegetables
grandfather house boy sausages door tree

Talk about people in the story

Can you choose the right words to finish each sentence?

...vegetables in the garden.

...her grandmother.

...sitting quietly with Lucky.

...the vegetables for their meals.

1.

Sara loves...

2.

Sara likes...

3.

Grandmother grows...

4.

Grandfather cooks...

What does Sara say?

Can you choose the right words for each picture?

A.

B.

C.

D.

Bruno wants to help.

Can I help?

Can I come with you?

Now can I help?

I think it's moving...

Can you choose the right sentence to go under each picture?

A. The turnip is moving now.

B. The turnip doesn't move.

C. They all fall down.

D. The turnip is moving a little.

1. Grandmother says, "One... two... three... PULL!"

...

2. Lucky pulls Bruno's tail.

...

3. A little mouse pulls Lucky's tail.

...

4. The turnip comes out of the ground.

...

Wrong words

There are four wrong words in the sentences below. Can you find them, and choose the right words?

Grandfather eats turnip every day for a year. He and Grandmother make turnip meals for all their children.

"I like turnips," says Grandmother, "but I want to cook something different next year."

Word list

around (prep) when you put your arms around something, you make a circle with your arms and hold it inside.

both (det) 'both' is used for two people or things. For example, "We both like dogs," or "Both those chairs are green."

chicken (n) a bird that lives on farms, and also the meat from that bird.

cook (n, v) when you cook food, you make it hot so that it is good to eat. Cooks are people who make food ready.

enormous (adj) very, very big.

fall down (v) when you can't stand, you fall down on the ground, for example when someone pushes you.

first (adv) before you do something else.

garden (n) a place where people grow flowers, fruit and vegetables.

mouse   turnip

vegetables

grow (v) when you grow flowers, fruit or vegetables, you put seeds in the ground and take care of the plants.

ground (n) the ground is under your feet. You stand or walk on the ground.

mouse (n) a very small animal with a long tail. Cats often chase mice.

pull (v) when you need to bring something heavy towards you with your hands, you pull it.

sausage (n) sausages are usually made with meat. They are long and round, and you cook them and eat them.

turnip (n) a kind of vegetable that grows under the ground and has long green leaves. Turnips are usually purple and white.

vegetable (n) vegetables grow on plants, above or under the ground. We eat vegetables.

cook

chicken

sausages

Answers

Can you see it in the picture?

Three things you can't see: boy, cat, sausages

Talk about people in the story

1. Sara loves her grandmother.
2. Sara likes sitting quietly with Lucky.
3. Grandmother grows vegetables in the garden.
4. Grandfather cooks the vegetables for their meals.

What does Sara say?

A. "Can I come with you?"
B. "Can I help?"
C. "Now can I help?"
D. "Bruno wants to help."

I think it's moving...

1. B
2. D
3. A
4. C

Wrong words

Grandfather <u>cooks</u> turnip every day for a <u>week</u>. He and Grandmother make turnip meals for all their <u>friends</u>.
"I like turnips," says Grandmother, "but I want to <u>grow</u> something different next year."

You can find information about other Usborne English Readers here: usborneenglishreaders.com

Designed by Vickie Robinson
Series designer: Laura Nelson Norris
Edited by Jane Chisholm
Digital imaging: John Russell

First published in 2021 by Usborne Publishing Ltd.,
Usborne House, 83-85 Saffron Hill, London EC1N 8RT, England.
usborne.com Copyright © 2021 Usborne Publishing Ltd.